LUCY DANIELS
Hedgehog Home

Illustrated by Paul Howard

Hodder
Children's
Books

a division of Hodder Headline plc

Special thanks to Susan Bentley

Text copyright © 1999 Ben M. Baglio
Created by Ben M. Baglio, London W12 7QY
Illustrations copyright © 1999 Paul Howard
Cover illustration by Chris Chapman

First published in Great Britain in 1998
by Hodder Children's Books

A Catalogue record for this book is available from the British Library

ISBN 0 340 73586 4

Typeset by Avon Dataset Ltd, Bidford-on-Avon, Warks

Printed and bound in Great Britain by
The Guernsey Press Co. Ltd, Channel Isles

Hodder Children's Books
a division of Hodder Headline plc
338 Euston Road
London NW1 3BH

Contents

1

A cold snap

"Mandy Hope! Are you ready to go?" Mrs Todd called. "Your gran will be here to fetch you soon."

"Oh." Mandy turned towards the rest of the class. She was putting a thick layer of bedding in the class gerbils' cage. "I've just about finished," she said to her teacher.

She closed the cage door, then put the bag of bedding back in the cupboard.

"Thank you, Mandy," Mrs Todd said with a smile. "At least Terry and Jerry won't notice that the central heating is broken!"

"Well *I've* noticed!" Gary Roberts said. "It's freezing!"

Everyone laughed. They were all wearing their coats and scarfs in class. It was so cold, you could see your breath.

It was Thursday morning. The heating hadn't been working since first thing that day. No one could mend it for a while, so the school was going to have to close early for half-term.

"If you were a gerbil, Mandy would make sure you were warm," Pam Stanton said. "She cares about animals more than people!"

Mandy grinned at her classmate. She did love animals. Both her parents were vets. She especially liked going home to see the new arrivals at Animal Ark.

"Can I go along to James Hunter's class, please?" she asked Mrs Todd. "My gran is taking him back to Lilac Cottage as well."

James was her best friend. He was in the year below her.

Mrs Todd glanced out of the classroom window. "There's your gran at the gate now.

You don't want to keep her waiting in this weather. All right, off you go and fetch James."

Mandy didn't move straight away. She looked at the gerbils' cage. "Is somebody taking Terry and Jerry home with them?" she asked.

"Animals again, Mandy?" Mrs Todd asked. "Don't worry. I'll take Terry and Jerry home with me today."

Mandy smiled. Mrs Todd liked animals, too. She had a spaniel called Jodie.

"That's all right then!" Mandy snatched up her schoolbag and headed for the door.

"Here you are, Mandy. I almost forgot," Mrs Todd said. "A letter from Mrs Garvie for your parents. It explains about the boiler breaking down."

Mrs Garvie was the headteacher at Welford Village Primary School. She had decided that children whose parents could meet them early could go home. Some of Mandy's classmates had been picked up already. But others, like Pam and Gary, would have to stay in class until home time.

"Lucky thing!" Gary said, as Mandy passed his desk. "I wish I could go home."

Mandy looked at Gary's glum face. "James

and I could meet you on the green tomorrow," she said. "It's an extra-long school holiday now!"

Gary cheered up. "Yeah! We could have a snowball fight! – or make snowmen!"

"Bye, Mrs Todd. Bye, everyone else!" Mandy called. "See you tomorrow afternoon, Gary."

Mandy made her way down the corridor. She saw James coming towards her. He must have spotted Gran waiting outside.

"Hi, Mandy!" he said, heaving his schoolbag on to his shoulder.

Gran was walking up the school path. It had begun snowing again. Big fluffy snowflakes tumbled over themselves before they settled on the frozen playground.

"Hello you two," said Gran. "I bet you're half-frozen. Come on; let's get back to Lilac Cottage. A hot lunch will soon warm you up."

"Great!" James said. He rubbed at his glasses, wiping away flecks of snow.

Mandy laughed. James loved visiting Lilac Cottage and he especially loved her gran's home cooking!

"Well, I don't expect you two mind that the heating's broken down!" joked Gran, as they

began walking along Church Lane.

Mandy shook her head. "No. We've got two extra days of half-term holiday! Lots more time to spend with Frisky."

Frisky was a hamster. He belonged to Gran's friend Mary. Mary had gone to stay with her sister, who had broken her hip a few weeks ago, and Mandy and James had been helping Gran look after the little animal. They had looked after Frisky once before, when Mary had gone on holiday.

"How is he today?" she asked Gran.

"He's fine," Gran said. "He's been asleep in his nest all morning."

"As usual!" laughed James.

Gran chuckled. "I expect he'll enjoy a visit from you two — when he wakes up."

Mandy's eyes shone. She was very fond of Frisky. The hamster seemed almost like her own pet. Pets weren't allowed at Animal Ark because her parents were too busy looking after *other people's* animals.

Mandy slipped off one of her gloves and dug around in her schoolbag. "Look. I've got a cardboard tube for Frisky to play with!"

"He'll love that!" said James. "I've brought a carrot. I found it in the bottom of the fridge. Do you think it's OK?" He held it up. "It looks a bit limp."

"I don't expect Frisky will notice," Mandy said with a chuckle. "He loves carrots."

"Well, you'd better make the most of your time with him, love," Gran said gently. "Mary phoned just before I left. Her sister's much better and Mary's niece is going to take over looking after her. Mary's planning to come home at the weekend."

"Oh." Mandy tried not to feel too disappointed. It was already Thursday. That meant they only had a few days left to spend with Frisky.

"Do you think hamsters have dreams?" Mandy asked, a short time later. She was looking at Frisky in his cage.

"I don't know," James said, with a grin. "But dogs do. Blackie twitches his nose and growls in his sleep!"

Mandy laughed. Blackie was James's Labrador puppy. He was lovely and friendly – but very naughty. James also had a pet cat – called Benji.

"At least Blackie can't get into trouble when he's asleep," she said.

"A good thing too!" laughed James. "Last night Dad found one of his best slippers in Blackie's basket. It was all chewed up."

"Uh-oh." Mandy chuckled. "Don't you mean his *ex*-best slippers?"

James nodded, grinning. "He's had to go back to wearing his scruffy old ones. He's *not* very amused."

They were upstairs in Lilac Cottage's spare bedroom. Frisky's cage was on a table near the radiator. Mandy could see the cosy nest Frisky had built. He was curled up inside. Just the teeniest bit of his brownish-grey fur was visible.

"Oh!" Mandy said. "I think he's waking up."

And he was. First a pointed nose poked out of the nest. Then two jet-black, shiny eyes appeared. Suddenly Frisky's round little body popped right out of the nest. He was much smaller than the golden hamsters that most people have. Mandy's dad had told her that Frisky was a Russian hamster.

Mandy put her finger through the bars of the cage and wriggled it. "Hello, Frisky!" she whispered, so she wouldn't startle him. "Isn't he lovely?"

James nodded. "Do you remember how your gran used to think he looked like a mouse?" he said, with a chuckle. "She wasn't sure if she liked him."

Mandy watched Frisky gnawing on a sunflower seed. "She does now that she's got used to him."

They gave Frisky bits of James's carrot. He crunched them up straight away.

"Shall we clean out his cage?" James suggested.

Mandy nodded. "There's probably time before lunch."

"We'll have to be careful we don't disturb his food store," said James.

Mandy nodded. She knew that hamsters hoarded food in the wild. Pet hamsters did the same thing. She put clean wood shavings into the cage, and James filled Frisky's water bottle.

"There!" Mandy said, putting the little china food bowl into the clean cage. "All spick and span. I'll just put this cardboard tube inside."

Frisky looked at them with his bright little eyes. Then he dashed across to his exercise wheel and began running as fast as he could.

The wheel whizzed round so fast it was almost a blur.

Mandy chuckled. "Look at him go! He'll be in that wheel for ages. He loves it so much."

"Mandy, James! Lunch is ready!" Gran called up the stairs.

"OK, Gran," Mandy answered, "We're coming!"

Mandy followed James out of the room. "We can come back later and let Frisky out to play for a little while," she said.

Gran was in the kitchen, pouring home-made soup into bowls. The radio was on and she was humming along to some music.

"Where's Grandad? Shall I go and fetch him?" Mandy asked.

"He'll be along in a minute, love," Gran said. "He's in the greenhouse – checking up on his fuchsias, I'd bet. He'd tuck those flowers up in bed if he could!"

Mandy laughed. Grandad was gardening-mad. He could grow anything and often won prizes for his flowers and vegetables at the Welford Show.

"I expect he's still fiddling with that old greenhouse heater," Gran said, piling crusty bread rolls on to plates. "He needs to buy a new one, but he won't hear of it."

Mandy grinned. "Yes, Grandad certainly gets attached to things."

"Attached?" Gran said. "Well, that's one word for it! I've tried to throw out his tatty old gardening sweater so many times, but he keeps rescuing it!"

Mandy and James laughed. Grandad was famous for hoarding things. A bit like Frisky really, Mandy thought!

Then they heard Grandad outside the door, stamping the snow from his boots. A moment later, he came into the kitchen. He winked at Mandy. "Your gran's been telling you all about my heater, hasn't she?"

He went over to the kitchen sink and began washing his hands.

"Oh, you heard me, did you?" Gran sounded a little annoyed. "That old heater is going to break any minute, Tom. Don't blame me if it packs up and your fuchsias freeze!"

Gran sometimes sounded fierce, but there was a twinkle in her eye.

"Now then, Dorothy," Grandad said mildly. "There's life in that old heater yet. Just like me! Is that leek and mushroom soup? Lovely. My favourite."

As they sat at the table to eat, the weather forecast came on the radio.

"Oh, dear," Gran said. "Just as I thought: more snow on the way. There'll be frost tonight."

Grandad looked concerned. "I think I'll go and check on Cowslip Cottage in the morning," he said. "I checked a few days ago, but it won't hurt to go again. There's always the risk of a burst water pipe."

Cowslip Cottage was where Gran's friend Mary lived. It was near Hobart's Corner, which was on the way to Animal Ark.

"Can we come with you, Grandad?" Mandy asked eagerly. "We want to visit Harold."

Harold was a hedgehog who lived in Mary's garden. Over the past weeks, Mandy and James had gone with Grandad when he checked on the cottage, and they had come to know the little animal quite well. They had seen him some evenings, searching the bushes for food.

Mandy had learnt that by February, most hedgehogs were beginning to come out of hibernation. But they would go back to sleep if the weather turned very cold again – just as it had recently.

"We-ell." Grandad stroked his chin. "Are you sure you can spare the time? I thought you two would be *far* too busy sledging!"

"Oh, no. We'd love to come, wouldn't we, James?" Mandy said.

James nodded.

"Because it's got so cold again, Harold's built himself a nest. It's in the space under the old apple tree's roots . . ." Mandy began. Seeing the broad grin on her grandad's face, she stopped.

Gran smiled. "Don't tease, Tom. You're just as interested in that hedgehog as Mandy is." Then she turned to Mandy. "He's always talking about him."

"Quite right too," Grandad said. "Hedgehogs are very good for the garden! I only wish one would move in here. It's slug city in the summer."

"Sounds like hedgehog heaven!" Mandy joked.

They all laughed.

"You can come along and see Harold, if you like," Grandad said. "But he might have gone back into hibernation."

Mandy nodded. "We'll come anyway."

"Right then, Mandy. I'll meet you at Animal Ark at nine sharp," Grandad said. "And we'll pick James up on the way."

"OK!" Mandy replied.

"Great!" James said. "Thanks for lunch, Mrs Hope. Shall we go back upstairs and let Frisky out to have a runaround, Mandy?"

She nodded. "Yes, there's ages yet before we have to go home . . . You know what?"

"Mmm?" said James.

Mandy grinned. "I'm going to love this extra-long school holiday!"

2

Hedgehog in danger

Mandy huffed and puffed as she pulled on her wellies the next morning.

"Having trouble?" her dad said, coming into the kitchen.

"*Oof!*" Mandy gave a final tug. "I'm ready now!"

"Just in time," said Mr Hope with a grin. "Here's Grandad now."

Grandad stamped his feet and rubbed his

hands together. He was all wrapped up against the cold. The tip of his nose was red and glowing. "Brrr! It's just like the Arctic outside. Worst weather we've had in years."

"Mandy tells me you're on hedgehog patrol today," Mr Hope said.

Mandy chuckled. "You mean *Harold* patrol!" She thought of the hedgehog, tucked up in his warm nest. If he *was* in hibernation again, he wouldn't notice the cold.

"Harold patrol . . . I like the sound of that!" Grandad laughed. "All set, Mandy? We'd better go and meet James now."

"Yep," Mandy replied. "Bye, Dad!"

"Have a good time!" Mr Hope said. "I'm off to Blackheath Farm to look at some sick chickens. See you later."

The snow crunched beneath Mandy's feet as she and Grandad made their way to the Hunters' modern house. It was close to the river, at the far end of Welford. James was at the window waiting. He ran straight out to meet them.

"Hi, Mandy. Hi, Mr Hope."

"Hello, James. No Blackie?" asked Grandad. James shook his head. "Dad took him out for a really long walk before he went to work. Blackie's curled up asleep in front of the fire."

"Quite right too. Young animals need their rest," Grandad said.

James nodded. "But he'll be ready for a walk this afternoon. I'll bring him with me then."

Mandy looked at James. "Why? where are you going this afternoon?"

"*We're* meeting Gary Roberts and some of the others on the green," James said. "Remember? It was your idea."

"Oh, yes!" Mandy grinned.

"She's had other things on her mind," Grandad explained. "Spiny things!"

They made their way to Hobart's Corner. Cowslip Cottage was a little way back from the road. Snow covered the roof and the front path. It looked just like a Christmas-cake decoration.

"Now, where's that front-door key?" Grandad was fishing in his pocket. He frowned, then put his head on one side. "Can you hear running water?"

Mandy listened hard. "I think so."

"I can hear it too," James added.

"Oh, dear." Grandad looked worried. "I

hope this isn't what I *think* it is."

He unlocked the door and pushed it open.

"Oh," Mandy gasped. Mary's sitting-room floor was under water. The sofa, chairs, table and electric heater all looked as if they were floating. There was water everywhere.

"Look!" James said. "It's even trickling down the stairs."

"Oh, my goodness!" Grandad rushed into the cottage. "A pipe's burst up in the roof space by the look of things. Mary hasn't got central heating – only that electric heater. Nothing's been keeping the pipes warm."

Mandy and James splashed into the sitting room after him.

"Oh dear," Grandad said. "Look at this kitchen. Water's poured under the back door too. The garden's probably awash as well."

Mandy stopped dead. "What about Harold's nest? The apple tree's just outside the back door."

James rushed to the window over the kitchen sink. "There are puddles of water all round it!"

Mandy had a sinking feeling in her stomach. "Come on, James. We've got to see if he's all right."

She turned the key in the back door, then tried to push it open. The door wouldn't budge.

"It's frozen shut," Grandad said. "You'll have to go round. Hang on a minute: I'll come with you. I'd better just turn the water off first."

Mandy waited impatiently while Grandad felt about under the sink. "You go ahead, Mandy," he said.

She dashed back through the cottage to the open front door. A few moments later, James followed her into the back garden.

"Oh." Mandy looked down worriedly at the roots. "We've got to scoop this wet snow away somehow. What can we use? Our gloves will be soaked in no time."

"How about these?" James held up two big serving spoons. "I borrowed them from Mary's kitchen!"

"James, you're brilliant!" Mandy told her friend.

Together they scooped up slushy snow and water. Then Mandy threw herself to her knees and plunged her hands into the puddle that was left. The cold made her shiver, but she took no notice. She was scared that Harold had drowned or been frozen inside his nest.

Then her fingers closed around a half–frozen ball of grass and leaves. "I've found the nest!" she said. Her heart was in her mouth. "Please be all right, Harold."

James leaned over to watch, as Mandy began easing the nest apart. "Is he all right?' he asked worriedly.

"I can't see him yet." Mandy worked her way carefully to the centre. She parted the last layer of tightly packed leaves.

"Oh no!" she cried. "It's empty."

"Empty?" James frowned. "But where can Harold have gone?"

Mandy leaped to her feet as she saw her grandad coming down the garden path.

"The water's off and I've phoned a plumber. He can't come out right away . . ." Grandad took one look at Mandy's face. "What is it, love?"

"It's Harold," Mandy said. "He's not in his nest!"

Grandad stroked his chin. "Perhaps the water flooding into his nest woke him up. I think I remember your dad saying that hedgehogs can swim."

"Oh, that must be it, then," Mandy said

eagerly. "Betty Hilder told me that hedgehogs wake from hibernation if they sense danger."

Betty Hilder ran the local animal sanctuary. She sometimes brought sick wild animals into Animal Ark.

"Wow! That's really clever," James said. "*Then* what do they do?"

"We-ell. I'm not sure exactly," Mandy admitted. "I think they look for somewhere warm and dry to build a new nest."

James glanced around Mary's garden. "Like . . . where?"

"James is right," Grandad said. "Harold's not going to be able to find a new place for his nest with all this snow and ice. And he'll freeze without shelter."

"Not if we find him," Mandy said. "He can't be far away."

"I'll go and look over here," James suggested.

While James checked under the snow-covered bushes, Grandad peered behind empty flowerpots. Mandy looked in the vegetable patch and behind the water barrel. But there was no sign of Harold.

Suddenly she gave a cry. "Look! Tracks in the snow!"

James and Grandad hurried over. "Well spotted," Grandad said.

The tracks led in a wavy line past Mary's garden shed. Mandy ran forward. Over by the fence, she saw a little dark shape – it was moving very slowly.

"It's Harold!" she burst out. "We've found him."

"Thank goodness!" Grandad said. "I was really worried about the little chap."

Mandy bent down and picked Harold up. "It's all right now," she said softly to him. "We'll look after you."

She cradled the hedgehog very gently against her coat, so she wouldn't alarm him. Harold lay stretched out on his side, his pointed face drooping downwards. He was soaking wet. Ice glistened on some of his spines, and he made no attempt to curl up.

"Oh! I think he's really sick," Mandy said.

"How do you know?" James asked.

"Hedgehogs only stay uncurled if they're very, *very* poorly," Mandy answered.

"He's hardly breathing," James said.

Then Harold blinked slowly and gave a shiver. Mandy felt a surge of hope. "I'll wrap him in my scarf: that'll warm him up a bit." She turned to her grandad. "We have to take him to Animal Ark. Mum will know what to do."

Grandad looked back towards Mary's cottage. "I really ought to see what I can do . . ." he said doubtfully.

"But we have to hurry, Grandad!" Mandy urged him. She felt close to tears. "Harold might die!"

Grandad looked down at him, all wrapped up in Mandy's multi-coloured scarf. "You're

right, love. The cottage will still be here later. Come on."

As soon as they reached Animal Ark, Mandy ran down the path and burst through the double doors. Seconds later, James and Grandad followed.

Jean Knox, the receptionist, looked up and smiled. "Hello, what's all the hurry?"

"It's an emergency," Mandy said. "Where's Mum?"

"She's in the examination room," Jean said. "You can go right in. There's ten minutes before the next appointment."

"There's no point James and me getting in the way," Grandad said. "We'll wait in the kitchen. OK, James?"

James nodded.

Mandy was already pushing open the door to the examination room. Mrs Hope was washing her hands at the sink. She turned and smiled. "Hello, Mandy," she said. "What have you got there: another stray?"

"It's Harold, the hedgehog from Mary's garden." Mandy gulped. "He's really sick, Mum."

"Put him on the table," Mrs Hope said

calmly. "You can tell me all about it while I examine him."

As Mandy unwrapped her scarf, she explained. Mrs Hope listened closely. She slipped on a pair of gloves, then picked Harold up very gently. He still made no attempt to curl up. He just lay there – eyes half-closed and legs sticking out at angles. Mandy could see the long fur on his soft, browny-grey belly.

"You're right, Mandy," Mrs Hope, after she had given Harold a thorough examination. "He's half-frozen, and in shock. But you

26

may have found him just in time."

Mandy managed a shaky smile. "What's going to happen now?"

"We'll give him some gentle warmth – just to bring him up to body heat," Mrs Hope said. "And start him on some fluids. I'm going to give him an injection for shock. There, that's done."

"Can I come with you to the unit?" Mandy asked. "I could help you."

Animals that were too sick to go home stayed in the unit. There was a small area at the back specially for wild animals.

"Come along then," Mrs Hope said. "As long as you only watch. You know the rules, love."

Mandy sighed, but she nodded. She wasn't allowed to help in the surgery until she was twelve. Three years to wait: it seemed like ages.

A few minutes later Harold was settled in. He lay stretched out beneath the red heating bulb hanging from his cage, his eyes closed.

"We've done all we can," Mrs Hope said. "Now it's just a matter of time."

"How *much* time?" Mandy asked.

"At least four or five hours," Mrs Hope told her.

"Oh. As long as that?" Mandy didn't think she could bear the suspense.

Mrs Hope gave her a brief hug. "Try not to worry, love. Hedgehogs are hardy little animals. Why don't you go and tell James and Grandad how he's getting on?"

"OK." Mandy pushed one finger through the bars and waggled it. "I'll see you later," she whispered.

Harold would survive. He just *had* to!

3

Snow pets

"That's morning surgery over with," Mrs Hope said to Mandy an hour or so later. "Ready for some lunch?"

Mandy helped her mum make cheese sandwiches.

"Would you put these on a plate in the fridge please, Mandy," Mrs Hope said. "Your dad can have them when he gets back from the riding stables."

Mrs Forsyth, who ran the stables, had a problem with one of her horses.

"I've just got to unpack some boxes of dressings," Mrs Hope said, when lunch was over. "Come and find me before you go out."

"OK, Mum," Mandy said. She sat at the kitchen table looking through a wildlife magazine, when a voice floated into the kitchen.

"Heel, Blackie!" James said firmly.

"Uh-oh." Mandy held her breath. Seconds later, there was a scrabbling sound at the back door.

"No, Blackie! *Stop* that!" James scolded.

Chuckling, Mandy opened the door. Blackie bounded inside, all big paws and happy wriggling body. James fell into the kitchen after him – he was hanging on to the end of Blackie's lead.

"He's never going to learn to behave," James grumbled, looking hot and cross.

"He will," Mandy said. "Training just takes time and patience."

"My dad says he'll have grey hair before Blackie walks at heel!" James said.

Blackie gave a short bark. Mandy bent down and gave the puppy a cuddle. "Never mind. Blackie's lovely just the way he is."

James smiled. Despite his complaints about Blackie's naughtiness, he adored his pet. "Yes, he is, isn't he?"

"Come on," Mandy said. "I have to find Mum before we go."

"Do you think she'd let us go and see Harold?" James asked.

Mandy smiled. "I'll ask her."

They found Mrs Hope in the treatment room. She was sorting packets of surgical dressing into sizes. She came out to speak to Mandy and James.

"Hello, you two," she said. "Or should I say, *three*!" She bent down and gave Blackie a friendly pat. "Are you just off to meet your friends?"

"Yes," Mandy said. "We wondered if we could see Harold before we go?"

Mrs Hope brushed back a curl of red hair. "Perhaps later, when he's stronger. Wild animals do best if they're not disturbed too much."

"All right, Mum," Mandy said. "See you later, then!"

"Bye, Mrs Hope," James said.

Blackie walked obediently beside James and Mandy as they trudged up the lane.

"He's not pulling against his lead!" James said, as pleased as anything. "I think he's starting to get the hang of things at last!"

"Good boy!" Mandy said to the puppy. "Perhaps *you're* getting the hang of training him too, James!" Secretly, she thought it was the thick snow that was slowing Blackie down. But she didn't say so to James.

A short time later they reached the village green. The huge oak-tree was heavy with snow and the pond was frozen.

Mrs McFarlane was outside the post office, sweeping the snow away from the shop doorway. She waved at Mandy and James. "My word," she called. "Blackie's training seems to be coming along a treat."

James flushed with pleasure.

A group of children were having a snowball fight near by. Mandy saw that Gary Roberts and Pam Stanton were with them, and she waved.

Suddenly a snowball came hurtling towards

her. She saw it coming and ducked. "Missed!"

The snowball zoomed past James and rolled a few centimetres in the snow. Blackie lurched forwards, pulling the lead out of James's hand. Growling and snapping, he jumped on the snowball.

"Uh-oh!" Mandy said. "Mrs McFarlane spoke too soon."

"He's just protecting me!" James said, looking embarrassed. "That's enough, Blackie. Come here!"

Blackie ignored him. He scampered round,

lead trailing. As he attacked the snowball, everyone laughed. Mrs McFarlane joined in. Mandy felt a bit sorry for James, and she was glad when Gary and Pam came over.

"You're lucky you can bring your pet with you," Gary said with a chuckle. "I can't play in the snow with Gertie!" Gertie was Gary's pet garter-snake.

"My Ginny's not much fun in the snow, either!" said Pam. She owned a guinea-pig.

"That's true," said James, cheering up.

"Shall we join in with the snowball fight?" Mandy asked James.

Before James could answer, Pam said, "We're bored with that now. Let's do something else."

"OK," said Gary. "What shall we do?"

"How about making snowmen?" Mandy said. "No, wait! We could make snow animals."

"Excellent!" Gary said. "I'm going to make a snake."

"That's a surprise," Pam said, with a grin. "Let's all make our pets!"

Gary and Pam ran off to start gathering up snow. Mandy hesitated. She hadn't got a pet – unless you counted all the sick animals that came into Animal Ark. Each of them was her friend, though, if only for a short while.

Which animal could she make? Then she had an idea. She hurried after the others.

Half an hour or so later, the snow animals were almost finished.

Gary's snake had come out well, although Mandy thought it looked a bit like a fat wavy sausage. Pam's guinea-pig was very realistic. It had little snowballs for ears and dug-out holes for eyes. And James's puppy *would* have been good, except that he had Blackie "helping" him!

Just then, James came over. "What's it supposed to be?" he asked, looking at Mandy's snow animal. "It's a bit like Pam's guinea-pig, but without the legs."

"Aha! You'll have to wait and see," Mandy said, giving the oval–shaped mound a final smoothover.

"It's got a point at the front. Is it going to be a fish?" asked James.

"It could be!" Mandy said mysteriously. "I have to add the finishing touches."

Then she went off across the village green to

find the things she needed. When she got back, Gary and Pam were standing with James. They were all looking down at her snow animal.

"None of us can guess what it is," Gary said.

Mandy smiled to herself. She dumped a pile of stones and twigs on to the snow. First she put two stones into place for eyes. Then she put a third stone at the pointed end of the oval-shape.

"That's its nose, isn't it?" Pam said. "But I still can't guess."

Mandy broke the twigs into short lengths. She began pushing them into the snow, starting a few centimetres back from the eyes.

James looked at the neat rows of twigs. "I know," he shouted. "It's Harold!"

Gary looked puzzled. "Looks like a hedgehog to me."

Mandy giggled. "Harold *is* a hedgehog!"

She told her classmates the saga: how Harold had nearly drowned, and then narrowly escaped being frozen.

"Oh!" Pam said. "The poor little thing. I hope he gets better."

"Me too," Mandy said.

Looking down at her snow hedgehog, she

began worrying about Harold all over again. She made up her mind to look in on him just as soon as she could.

"Your snow animal is easily the best, Mandy," James said. "I wonder how long these will last. If it stays cold, they could be here for days."

Mandy gave a chuckle as she saw Blackie heading straight for her snow hedgehog. "I should think mine's going to last about another five minutes!"

"Oh no!" James tried to head Blackie off!

Thinking it was a game the puppy darted round him. Blackie gave a short bark. He jumped about. He leaped in the air . . . and came down smack in the middle of the snow hedgehog. Snow and sticks flew everywhere. Blackie snorted as snow went up his nose. His whole body looked as if it had been dipped in flour.

Everyone laughed until their sides ached. With Blackie around, there was never a dull moment!

Mandy and James decided to call into Lilac Cottage before they went home.

Grandad was in the sitting-room, reading a gardening magazine.

"Any adverts in there for new heaters, Tom?" Gran asked cheekily from the doorway.

"Very funny, Dorothy," he answered. "My old heater's holding up just fine. So how's Harold doing, Mandy?"

"It'll be a few hours before we'll know if he's going to get better," Mandy replied.

Grandad got up and put his arm round her. "Don't look so worried," he said. "That little chap's a fighter. You'll see. What have you two been up to?"

Mandy and James told them about Blackie and the snow hedgehog.

"Dear me!" Grandad chuckled. "I hope that pup's behaviour improves before he's much older."

"Or before your raspberries are ready next year!" Mandy said.

James looked embarrassed. Mandy's grandad had fished Blackie out of his raspberry canes more than once.

"I'm just going to make some hot chocolate," Gran said. "Would you and James like some before you go up and see Frisky? I checked on him a moment ago. He's fast asleep."

"What a surprise!" James said.

After they finished their hot chocolate, Mandy and James went upstairs.

"Listen to that," James said. "Frisky's awake now."

They could hear him before they entered the spare room. His wheel was squeaking like mad as he whizzed round in it!

Mandy enjoyed watching Frisky playing with his toys, but she couldn't stop thinking about Harold. "I think I'd better go back to Animal Ark now," she said, after they had cleaned Frisky's cage.

"I have to go now anyway," James said. "I told Mum I would be home before it got dark."

Back at Animal Ark, Mandy dumped her boots and coat in the kitchen. Then she dashed straight into the modern vets' extension at the back.

Suddenly she skidded to a halt. "Oh, hi, Dad!" she said. "Sorry! Nearly bumped into you."

Mr Hope grinned. "I think I can guess where *you're* going in such a hurry. Still worried about Harold?"

Mandy nodded. "Can I see him yet?" When her dad hesitated, she said, "Oh, please, Dad!"

"Hmm." Mr Hope stroked his beard. "I'm just about to go and check on him. Come on. Only, you must be *really* quiet."

"Thanks, Dad." Mandy grinned from ear to ear. "I'll be as quiet as a mouse."

In the unit, Mandy watched her dad open Harold's cage. The hedgehog hadn't moved position. He lay stretched out, his pointed chin resting on the cage bottom.

"Oh," Mandy whispered. "He hasn't even touched his bowl of water."

"No." Mr Hope picked Harold up gently. "He doesn't look good. I'm going to have to give him some fluids," he said to Mandy in a soft voice, as he began to make up some baby-milk formula.

"Why don't you give him ordinary milk?" Mandy whispered.

"It's not good for hedgehogs, unless it's diluted well," Mr Hope explained. "Goat's or sheep's milk is good, and this baby-milk formula is ideal."

Mandy watched silently as her dad fed Harold

with a syringe. Harold coughed and sneezed, but he did swallow.

"Well – he's taken that milk," Mr Hope said. "But he's not out of the woods yet. We'll know one way or the other by the morning."

4
Good news

On Saturday morning Mandy jumped out of bed and quickly pulled on her jeans and sweater. Hurrying downstairs, she went straight to the unit.

Simon, the practice nurse, was already in there, giving the animals their medicine. "Hi, Mandy," he said. "You look like a girl on a mission!"

Simon had short fair hair and round glasses.

He had a serious face, but he was always making jokes. Mandy liked him.

"Hi," she said with a grin. "I've come to see how Harold is."

"Come on through," Simon said. "I was just about to check on him."

Her heart thumping, Mandy followed Simon through to the backroom. "Is he any better?"

Simon smiled. "See for yourself. Your dad's already looked him over."

"Oh!" Mandy breathed. She looked into the cage. "He seems much better!"

Harold was snuffling around, his little clawed feet scrabbling at the wood shavings. His eyes were bright as beads. The bowl of baby-milk formula that Mandy's dad had left in the cage was empty and it lay upside down.

"The cheeky thing! He's pushed it over!" She chuckled. "Maybe that's hedgehog language for 'food, please'!"

"You could be right!" Simon said. "Food coming up. Vet's orders!"

Mandy watched as Simon opened a tin of cat food. He forked some into a bowl and put it in the cage. Harold didn't hesitate. His nose twitched once, twice — then he scurried forward and stuck his head in the bowl.

"He's really tucking in!" Mandy said. She looked up at Simon, her eyes shining. "I must go and tell James the good news."

James was waiting by himself outside Lilac Cottage when Mandy arrived. They had arranged to go with her grandparents to Cowslip Cottage.

"Hi, James. Where's Blackie?" Mandy asked. James usually took his pet everywhere.

"Mum said it was best to leave him at home,"

James answered, looking gloomy. "She said Blackie plus a flooded cottage was a recipe for disaster!"

Mandy grinned. She loved Blackie dearly, but she had to agree. "I've got some brilliant news!" she said. "Harold's going to be fine!"

"Great!" James cheered up. "Let's go inside. I want to hear all about it!"

Gran opened the door with a smile. "Hello, you two. You're bright and early."

Grandad was reading his newspaper at the kitchen table. He put it away when he saw Mandy and James.

"Guess what!" Mandy said. "Harold's much better. He's eating like a horse!"

Grandad chuckled. "Quite a feat for a hedgehog!" He winked at her. "I told you the little chap was a fighter."

"Mmm," she said. "But how did you know?"

Grandad put his head on one side. "Oh, I know a thing or two," he said.

"Pity you don't know it's time to throw out that old heater," Gran muttered.

Mandy burst out laughing. "He'll never do *that*!"

"Hrrmph!" Grandad got up from his chair. "I'd better drive over to Cowslip Cottage. I've got to let the plumber in. Are you ready to come with me?"

"Oh," Mandy hovered anxiously near the door. "We were just about to clean Frisky out."

Gran smiled. "Pets must come first." She turned to her husband. "We'll walk over and meet you in a bit, Tom."

Mandy and James went up to the spare room. Frisky was awake and chewing on a piece of apple wood. He turned his head and peered at them with his bright beady eyes.

"He looks lively," Mandy said. "I wonder if he'd like to come out for a while."

She opened the cage door, and slowly put her hand inside. Frisky hesitated, then hopped on to her palm. Mandy held her breath. She lifted him out carefully.

"Wow! That's the first time he's ever done that!" James said. "Usually you have to pick him up."

"Well, he *is* pretty used to both of us now." Mandy flushed with pleasure. Having an animal who would trust you was the best feeling in the world.

She was going to miss Frisky when he moved back into Cowslip Cottage with Mary. But Mary couldn't move back yet – the cottage was so cold and damp, perhaps Frisky would be staying on a bit longer with Mandy's gran and grandad. She hoped so.

Suddenly Frisky ran up Mandy's arm. He sat on her shoulder, then ducked inside the neck of her sweater. Mandy kept perfectly still. It tickled as Frisky ran down her back and around her waist. A moment later, Frisky popped out of her cuff. Mandy drew him gently into her cupped hands.

"Would you like to hold him now, James?" she asked.

"Yes, please!" James held out his hands eagerly.

While James played with Frisky, Mandy cleaned out the cage and saw to his food and water.

Frisky was sitting in James's track-suit pocket. James took him out and put him in his cage. "There you go," he said. "See you later."

"He's not listening!" Mandy said with a grin. "Look. He's stuffing his cheek pouches with hamster mix!"

James chuckled. "Careful, Frisky. Mandy's gran will think you have mumps again!"

They were still laughing when they came into the kitchen. Gran was packing sandwiches and a Thermos flask into a basket. "What's the joke?" she asked.

When they told her she began laughing as well. "Fancy me making that mistake! I knew nothing about hamsters the first time Mary left him here. Now I'm quite an expert – thanks to my two friendly hamster-keepers!"

Half an hour later, Mandy, James and Gran arrived at Cowslip Cottage. Grandad was outside: he was just waving goodbye to the plumber as he drove off in his van.

As Gran entered the cottage, water splashed around her feet. "Oh, my goodness!" she exclaimed. "It's much worse than I thought."

Grandad came into the sitting-room. He held up a mop and bucket. "Right, troops!" he said. "Ready for action?"

The next couple of hours rushed by. Mandy and James helped clear all the water out of the sitting-room. Gran got busy filling black plastic sacks with soggy rugs and drenched curtains.

"Phew!" James said, pausing to take a breath. "All this work is making me hungry."

Mandy grinned. "But you're *always* hungry!"

"James is right. Time for a break," Gran said. She unpacked her basket and laid out the food. "Tuck in: there's plenty to go round."

Mandy munched on an egg and cress sandwich. "Mmm, lovely! Thanks, Gran," she said.

"Thanks, Mrs Hope," James added, wiping egg off his chin.

When they'd finished eating, they began

work again. A couple of Mary's neighbours arrived, and they brought extra mops and buckets. By the middle of the afternoon the floors were almost dry.

Gran stood with her hands on her hips. She shook her head. "It's still a mess. We'll have to come back tomorrow. Mary was all for dashing straight back home when I phoned her, but I said we'd take care of everything."

"So when's she expected back?" asked one of the neighbours.

"Some time on Monday now," Gran replied. "A couple of days later than she'd planned. Her niece can't get to her sister's to take over until then. Mary obviously can't leave her sister alone."

"No. Of course not," the neighbour said. "Monday? That's only the day after tomorrow. The cottage will still be damp and chilly."

"What about Frisky?" James asked Mandy. "He can't come back here, can he?"

"No." Mandy shook her head. "Hamsters have to be kept warm. They get sick if they get cold and wet."

"Same as people!" Grandad added. "This is no place for human or hamster!"

"Quite right," Gran said. "That's why I told Mary she can come and stay with us."

Gran and Grandad dropped Mandy off at Animal Ark just before teatime.

"Thanks for the lift, Grandad!" Mandy called as they drove off. "Bye, James!"

"See you at the big clean-up tomorrow!" James called back.

Mandy bumped into her dad in the kitchen. His white vet's coat was hung over a chair. "Just putting some potatoes in to bake," he explained, giving her one of his special crooked grins.

Mandy smiled. Dad often made supper when her mum was out doing the calls. He wasn't very organised, but his meals usually turned out all right.

"So how did the mop-up go?" Mr Hope asked.

"It was hard work," Mandy told him. "We still haven't finished. Gran's hired a machine. A dee-hew . . . something."

Mr Hope chuckled. "A dehumidifier. It's a drying-out machine. It sucks water out of the air." He put his white coat back on. "I'm just popping back into the unit to check on a new arrival – a puppy. Want to come along? You can visit Harold at the same time."

"Yes, please!" Mandy said.

Mr Hope laughed. "As if I needed to ask!"

The spaniel puppy was asleep in his cage. Mandy went to look. "He's lovely. What's wrong with him?" She always felt sad at the thought of animals being ill.

"He'd swallowed a piece of bone," Mr Hope explained, "and it got stuck in his throat. A small operation put it right. He'll be fine now."

Mandy would have loved to give the puppy a cuddle. But she knew that you didn't disturb animals when they were sleeping.

"Let's have a look at Harold," Mr Hope said. "It's time I weighed him."

Harold was curled into a tight ball of spines in the corner. Mandy could see his deep, even breaths. His empty food dish was upside down again. Suddenly, he looked up, nose twitching and eyes blinking.

Mr Hope opened the cage. He lifted Harold out carefully and put him on the scales. "Hmm. He's lost a bit of weight through hibernation. But that's natural."

"I think he wants some more cat food," Mandy said. "Look, he's turned his dish over again!"

Mr Hope smiled. "Hedgehogs often do that. It's one way you know for sure who's visiting the food you leave out in your garden."

Mr Hope filled Harold's dish with some more cat food. As soon as he was back in his cage, Harold rushed straight over to it.

"Gosh," Mandy said, "he's nearly smacking his lips!"

"He's got a good appetite. Just like me!" Mr Hope joked. "At this rate, he'll be back up to a good weight in a day or two."

"Then can we let him go?" Mandy asked.

Mr Hope nodded. "He's a fine big chap. Ideally, he ought to go back into Mary's garden. That's his territory."

"But it's full of ice and snow," Mandy said.

"That's right," her dad said. "So how about if we contact Betty Hilder? Harold can live at the wildlife sanctuary until Mary's garden thaws out."

"Oh." Mandy frowned. She didn't like to think of Harold going to the sanctuary. She thought Mary would miss having Harold around.

Mr Hope looked at Mandy. "What is it, love? Have you got another idea for Harold?"

Mandy thought for a moment. "I might have. I'll let you know!"

5
Mandy's idea

Mandy phoned Grandad as soon as she could. Her heart began to race: what if he didn't like her idea?

"Grandad," she pleaded, "I've got something to ask you."

"That sounds suspicious," Grandad said. "Go on, then. I'm all ears."

"It's about Harold," Mandy began. "You know he hasn't got anywhere to live? Well —

Dad's going to phone Betty Hilder. But I thought Mary would miss Harold if he went to live at the animal sanctuary. So, I wondered if Harold could maybe . . . live in your garden? It would be *really* good. Because Gran said Mary will be staying at Lilac Cottage as well! She wouldn't miss Harold at all," she finished all out of breath.

"Goodness me!" Grandad said, with a chuckle. "That was quite a speech."

"Yes," Mandy panted. "But can he, Grandad? *Can* he live in your garden?"

"Of course he can!" Grandad said. "I'd like nothing more than to help the little chap out. But I might need both your and James's help."

"We'd love to help!" Mandy said. "I'll go and tell Dad not to phone Betty Hilder."

"You do that," Grandad said. "But don't say anything to your gran yet, will you? I want it to be a surprise."

"OK," Mandy agreed. She hoped she'd remember. She found it hard keeping any news about animals to herself. "Where do you think Harold should make his nest?"

"Hmm." Grandad sounded thoughtful. "It will have to be somewhere warm and safe."

"And dry," Mandy added. "No more floods!"

"*Definitely* no more floods! Tell you what," Grandad said, "leave it with me. By tomorrow, I'll have thought of the perfect place."

As soon as Grandad had put down the phone, Mandy phoned James and told him all about her plan. "And Grandad *really* wants to help Harold. He's going to think of the best place for his nest!"

"Wow!" James said. "Lucky old Harold. Lilac Cottage's garden must have heaps of places for him to build a nest."

"Yes," Mandy agreed. "I can't wait to see what Grandad comes up with."

"Yoo-hoo!" called a voice behind Mandy and James.

There were making their way to Lilac Cottage early the following morning. James had Blackie with him.

Mandy turned round. "It's Mrs Ponsonby."

A large lady swept towards them. She was wearing a fluffy coat and a pink woolly hat. Pandora, her Pekinese, was tucked under one arm.

"Hello, Mrs Ponsonby," Mandy and James chorused.

"Out for an early stroll?" Mrs Ponsonby asked. She peered down at Blackie. "That puppy ought to be wearing a coat. Like my darling Pandora."

Pandora blinked at Mandy and James with black, boot-button eyes. Mandy looked at the little dog. Pandora wore a fluffy yellow coat.

"It's all right, Mrs Ponsonby," James said politely. "All this exercise keeps Blackie warm. He loves playing in the snow."

And he's already wearing a coat — his own thick black one, Mandy thought. "Does *Pandora* like playing in the snow, Mrs Ponsonby?" she asked.

Mrs Ponsonby shook her head. "Oh, I'd never allow that. Her tiny tootsies would get frozen. Wouldn't they, darling?" she cooed to the little dog.

Pandora gave a yap, then yawned. She snuggled against her owner and closed her eyes. "Are you tired, my precious?" Mrs Ponsonby asked. "We'd best be off, then." She gave Mandy and James a cheery wave as she moved away. Her voice floated back to them: "Come along, Pandora. Time for your warm milk, then you can have your nap."

Mandy and James smiled. Pandora had to be the most spoiled dog in Welford.

Blackie gave a short bark. He jumped up, snowy paws scrabbling at Mandy's jeans. Mandy patted his head. "Blackie doesn't think much of the idea of warm milk and a nap!"

"No. He'd rather have a dog biscuit and a walk any day!" James laughed. "Come on, Blackie."

As they reached Lilac Cottage, they saw Grandad in the drive. He had been clearing away the previous night's snow. "Hello there!" he said, banging snow off his brush. "Come into the back garden. I've found just the place for Harold."

"But what about Gran?" Mandy whispered. "Won't she see us?"

"It's all right. She had to go out," Grandad explained. "One of her ladies is ill, so she's doing the church flowers."

Gran was chairwoman of Welford Women's Institute. The ladies took turns to organise fresh flower arrangements for the church and had won lots of prizes. "Gran's arrangements are always ginormous!" Mandy said.

"Ginormous?" Grandad laughed. "That's the right word for them! How's Harold this morning – you did check up on him?"

Mandy grinned. "Of course! He ate a big tin of cat food yesterday – all by himself! Dad says he'll be back to normal in no tine."

"That's wonderful news." Grandad had stopped walking. "Well – what do you think?"

Mandy stared. They were standing at the top of the vegetable garden. She saw the big fenced area around the compost heap. Everything was covered by a thick layer of snow.

"But – where's Harold going to live?" she asked.

"Right there," Grandad said, pointing. "Under my compost heap!"

"That's perfect," Mandy grinned, remembering that hedgehogs loved to bury themselves in compost heaps. "That's perfect."

Suddenly Blackie rushed forward. He bounded on to the snow-covered heap, and in a flash he was on top. He gave a short bark.

"Blackie! Come down!" James said.

Blackie ignored him. He flicked up the powdery snow with his front paws.

Mandy couldn't help laughing. James tried so hard to make Blackie behave, but it just didn't work.

Grandad chuckled. "I think Blackie approves of Harold's new home!" He went to his shed and pushed open the door. "Come in for a moment. I've got something else to show you."

Blackie was inside the shed like a shot. He nosed around among the flowerpots and garden tools, his tail wagging. James looked a bit worried. "Blackie, come away!"

"He's all right," Grandad said. "Anything that might hurt him is out of reach." He picked up an old wooden crate. "Do you think we could find a use for this?"

"It might make a cosy home for a hedgehog," Mandy said.

"That's just what I thought." Grandad looked pleased. "We'll bury it under the compost heap. Here you are; have a trowel each. There's no time like the present!"

Back at the compost heap, they all got busy. Grandad dug out spadefuls from the bottom of the heap, then Mandy and James used their trowels to make the space bigger.

"It's all brown and crumbly inside here,"

Mandy said. She had expected to find lots of grass and weeds.

"Yes, that's right," Grandad said. "Just like good compost should be. It's grand stuff. You could slice it up and put it in your sandwiches."

"Ugh!" Mandy pulled a face. Then she noticed the twinkle in Grandad's eye. "Oh, Grandad!"

"It's not frozen inside here," James said, digging in further with his trowel.

Mandy took off her glove and felt the compost. "It feels quite warm."

"Compost heaps are always warm inside," Grandad explained. "As things rot down, they give out heat. Harold will be snug as a bug inside here."

When the space was big enough, Grandad picked up the crate.

"It's got a round hole in one side," Mandy said. She hadn't noticed that before.

"Is that *supposed* to be there, Mr Hope?" James asked.

"Oh, yes. I put it there on purpose. You'll see why in a minute." Grandad put the crate, open end down, inside the space. Then he produced a length of old plastic drainpipe.

Mandy's eyes widened. What could Grandad have in mind?

"We wedge one end of the pipe into the side of the crate. Like this," Grandad said. "Then we bury the rest, and leave just the end sticking out."

Mandy was puzzled. "But . . . what for?"

"I think I know!" James burst out. "It's Harold's special doorway to his nest! Nothing bigger than a hedgehog could get in."

"Oh, yes!" Mandy said. "That's *really* clever, Grandad!"

"I'm glad you think so," Grandad said, with a chuckle. "But it's Harold we have to convince."

"He'll love it," Mandy said. "I just know he will."

James grinned. "I would. If I was a hedgehog, that is!"

"Grandad . . . ?" Mandy had a worrying thought. "Could Harold get stuck in that pipe?"

He shook his head. "I checked on that. As long as the pipe's at least twelve centimetres across, it's fine. Hedgehogs can flatten their spines down and squeeze into really small spaces."

Mandy was impressed. "Grandad? How did you . . . ?" she began. "Oh, I bet Dad gave you one of our leaflets about looking after hedgehogs!"

"Spot on! You caught me out." Grandad smiled. "And I popped over to the Welford Animal Sanctuary the other day. That's where I saw the trick with the drainpipe. Betty fixes them to old rabbit hutches for her hedgehogs. It was Betty who suggested the compost heap."

Mandy smiled to herself. Grandad had gone

to a lot of trouble for Harold. He certainly was fond of the little animal.

It didn't take long to pack the compost back around the box. Very soon, just the end of the pipe could be seen.

"Harold's going to *love* his new home," Mandy said. She wished they could go and fetch him — that very second!

6

A surprise for Gran

"Now, remember," Grandad whispered ten minutes later, as they heard the front door open. "Not a word to your gran."

They were all sitting around the kitchen table. Mandy and James were sipping hot drinks.

"Hello, everyone!" Gran said, coming into the kitchen. She put her basket by the back door. "Are you waiting for me?"

"Er, yes," Grandad said. "We're all ready to go and do some more cleaning at Cowslip Cottage."

Mandy tried to keep a straight face, but it wasn't easy. Every time she thought of Harold's new home, she wanted to smile. Gran *was* going to get a surprise!

"Well, you *are* keen!" Gran gave them a suspicious look. She smiled. "I'll just go and change."

"Phew," Mandy said, as Gran went out of the kitchen. "I think she knows something's going on."

"I'm sure she does," Grandad said. "Don't worry. We won't keep her in suspense much longer!" He put on his coat. "I'll go and put the cleaning things in the car."

Gran reappeared a few minutes later. She had changed into an old track suit. "All set?"

Mandy and James nodded. They reached for their coats. Blackie gave a short bark. "He says he's ready, too," James said.

Gran reached down and gave him a pat. "You'll have to make sure Blackie behaves," she said to James. "There's still a lot of mess in Mary's cottage."

"I will, Mrs Hope," James promised. "I'll put him on his lead now."

Blackie sat between Mandy's and James's feet for the short drive to Cowslip Cottage. Once there, they all piled out of the car. Gran unlocked the cottage door while Grandad fetched the box of cleaning things.

"It smells a bit funny in here," James said, standing in Mary's kitchen.

Gran was rolling up her sleeves. "It's all this damp furniture. Things will be better after a good clean-up. I'll just get organised."

Grandad, meanwhile, went into the sitting-room. Mandy and James followed him.

On the bare stone floor there sat a strange, square-shaped machine. It had a plastic panel on top, and red and black control knobs. A faint whirring noise came from it. Someone had placed a bucket beneath the spout on its side.

"Crikey!" James said, pushing his glasses up his nose. "What's that?"

"It's something from Mars!" Mandy joked.

James made a wobbly-voiced alien noise, and they both fell about laughing. Blackie gave a low growl and threw himself down on to his front paws, his tail wagging madly.

"Very funny, you two! That's the dehumidifier," Grandad said. "Make sure Blackie doesn't attack it, James!" He bent over the machine. "Ah, it's working. Look, this bucket's almost full of water. I'll just go and empty it."

A few minutes later, Gran appeared wearing an apron. "Right, who wants a job?"

For the next two hours, floors were scrubbed and walls were wiped. Grandad brought down the bedroom carpets and stacked them outside the back door.

"This is harder work than yesterday!" James said, pushing his fringe out of his eyes.

At last Gran was satisfied. "Well – it smells fresher now, but it's still so damp in here. Pity we can't put the electric heater on. That would have helped dry things out. Still, Mary will be warm and snug in our spare bedroom."

"With Frisky," Mandy said. "He'll be company for her."

"That's right, Mandy," Gran said. "Frisky will help her feel at home . . . Oh, dear. I've just had a thought."

"What's that?" Grandad asked.

Gran looked worried. "Mary's going to be upset enough about her cottage, without worrying about Harold being sick at Animal Ark."

"Don't worry, Gran. Harold's going to—" Mandy began.

"Be better soon. Isn't he, Mandy, love?" Grandad finished quickly, catching her eye. "Isn't that what you were about to say?"

"Oh, er, yes," Mandy said, suddenly realising her mistake.

"That's good," Gran said. "Poor Harold. He's homeless, just like Mary. What a shame . . ." She looked thoughtful.

"I think I'll just pop back to Lilac Cottage, Dorothy," Grandad said quickly, putting his coat on. "I can start moving some of that stuff out of the spare room. Otherwise, Mary won't even get *into* it! Do you want to come with me, Mandy? You can keep an eye on Frisky?"

Mandy nodded. Grandad was up to something. What could it be?

Mandy was in Grandad's car. She looked across at him. "Grandad, why are we going back to Lilac Cottage?"

"Not to get the bedroom ready!" he chuckled. "That was an excuse. I've just remembered – there are some spaces in the fence around the compost heap. I want to block them off before Harold moves in."

"Oh yes," Mandy said. "Hedgehogs can crawl under fences."

"That's right," Grandad nodded. "This won't take two ticks. Then we'll pop back and pick up your gran."

Mandy grinned. Grandad was really looking forward to surprising Gran about Harold.

Back at Lilac Cottage, Grandad fetched his tool kit. Mandy helped carry some small pieces of wood, then she held them steady while Grandad worked.

"That's it. Watch your fingers," Grandad warned, as he hammered in a nail.

"Almost finished," Mandy said, twenty minutes later.

Suddenly a small black figure shot down the garden path. It leaped on Mandy, and she fell over backwards in the snow. Blackie placed two paws on her chest and licked her face.

"Oof! Stop it!" Mandy giggled, trying to get up.

She rolled over — and saw James and Gran looking down at her. They had walked back from Cowslip Cottage.

"*Uh-oh*," Mandy said, as she scrambled to her feet.

"That's let the cat out of the bag!" James said, as he put the lead on Blackie.

"Whatever's going on here?" Gran said. She stood with her hands on her hips, a twinkle in her eye. "Tom . . . ?"

Grandad looked sheepish. He held the hammer behind his back. "Oh . . . er, hello, Dorothy. We didn't hear you arrive."

"No, you were too busy," Gran agreed, looking at the fence.

Mandy shifted her feet. "We'd better tell her, Grandad."

"Tell me what?" Gran said. "Has this got something to do with you, Mandy?"

Mandy nodded. "It's about Harold. He needed a home. And — well — I asked Grandad if he could help. It was going to be a surprise for you . . ." She stopped. Gran had begun to laugh!

"How funny," Gran said, wiping her eyes. "I was going to suggest that Harold came to live in our garden. But you beat me to it, Mandy!"

Mandy started laughing too. Then James and Grandad joined in.

"And there I was, trying to keep it a secret!" Grandad said.

"Well, you wanted a hedgehog to move in, Tom," Gran said. "Seems like you've got your wish!"

"Yes," Mandy chuckled. "Even if Harold is only a hedgehog-on-loan!"

7

Harold moves in

Gran made them a huge Sunday lunch. "You've all earned it," she said, "after working so hard at Mary's cottage."

After they'd all eaten, Mandy and James helped wash-up.

"Right, that's finished." Gran took off her apron. "Have you got any plans for this afternoon?"

Mandy dried her hands. "I thought James

and I might go back to Animal Ark."

"To check on Harold," James added.

Mandy nodded. "We *might* be able to bring him back here."

"That would be great!" James said.

Gran chuckled. "You two seem very keen to get that hedgehog into his new home!"

"We are, Gran!" Mandy said. "Anyway — Harold won't want to stay in the unit if he's better."

"That's true," Gran agreed. "Grandad will run you there. Ask him when he comes in from the greenhouse. He's checking up on his fuchsias — again."

Mandy grinned. "Is his old heater still working?"

Gran sighed. "For the moment!"

Mandy and James laughed. Grandad really did love his fuchsias. He checked them every night and every morning.

"I don't know what he gets up to in that greenhouse," Gran said. "He'll probably be out there for another half an hour at least."

"Shall we go up and see to Frisky while we're waiting?" James suggested.

"Good idea!" Mandy made for the stairs.

With Mary coming home tomorrow, they wanted to make sure that Frisky's cage was extra spick and span.

"Blackie can stay with me," Gran said. "He'll keep me company while I write a few letters. Come along, boy!"

Blackie gave a short bark. He scampered into the sitting-room and flopped down beside the writing-desk. Wagging his tail, he looked up at Gran.

"How *does* she do that?" James asked in amazement.

"Gran says she's got a secret weapon," Mandy said.

"What's that then?" James said, frowning. "Maybe she'd like to lend it to me!"

Mandy laughed. "It's not that kind of a weapon. She puts a few dog biscuits in the desk drawer!"

"Just think," James said. "Tomorrow is Monday. The first *real* day of the school holiday." He was tipping hamster mix into Frisky's food bowl.

"A whole week left!" Mandy said. "It seems like we've already been off for ages – loads of things have happened."

James nodded. "Lucky for us that the school heating broke down."

"Yes!" Mandy agreed. She liked school, but she liked having all this time to spend with animals even more. She filled Frisky's water bottle, then looped it on the side of the cage. "There – finished. And Frisky didn't even wake up!"

They crept out of the bedroom and went downstairs. Grandad was in the kitchen, and he looked up as they came in. "Gran says you'd like a lift to Animal Ark," he said.

"Yes, please," Mandy said.

He picked up his car keys. "Come on then."

"Where's Blackie?" Mandy asked.

Grandad chuckled. "Asleep under your gran's desk."

"He's probably full of dog biscuits!" James whispered to Mandy.

As Mandy went into Animal Ark, a few minutes later, Mrs Hope came out of the sitting-room. She was wearing a loose top and leggings; her red hair tied back.

"Hi, Mum," Mandy said. "Are you practising your yoga?"

"Yes." Mrs Hope smiled. "But I'm nearly finished."

"Is Dad here?" Mandy asked.

Mrs Hope shook her head. "He's been called out to an emergency up at Syke Farm. A pregnant ewe has slipped on the ice: it looks like she's going into premature labour."

"Oh." Mandy's face fell. "The poor thing." She knew that Dora Janeki ran Syke Farm. Mandy hoped the ewe and lamb would both be all right.

Mrs Hope patted her arm. "Don't worry, love. Your dad will do his best." She looked at James and Grandad, then back at Mandy. "Why do I have a feeling this isn't a social visit?"

Mandy brightened. "We've come about Harold,"

"Mr Hope's made him a brilliant home in his compost heap," James said.

"It really is lovely," Mandy added. "It's got a proper hedgehog entrance and everything."

"Sounds perfect," Mrs Hope said.

"We were wondering," Mandy rushed on, "if we might be able to take Harold back to Lilac Cottage – so he can move in."

Mrs Hope was listening with amusement. "Right now?" She looked at Grandad.

"Well." Grandad coughed. "Only if the little chap is a hundred per cent fit."

"I know it's your day off and everything . . ." Mandy pleaded.

"But you want me check him over?" Mrs Hope laughed. "That hedgehog certainly has a lot of people looking out for him!"

"Quite right too, Emily," Grandad said. "He's a very brave little chap."

"I won't argue with that." Mrs Hope put her arm round Mandy's shoulders. "All right. Come through to the unit. But I'm not making any promises — understand?"

Mandy nodded.

"Good girl." Mrs Hope looked at Grandad. "Why don't you and James put the kettle on, Dad? We won't be long."

In the unit, Mandy went straight up to Harold's cage. "I think he's asleep," she said, looking at the spiny bundle half-covered with torn-up newspaper.

"Yes," Mrs Hope said. "Hedgehogs are most active at night-time."

"Just like Frisky," Mandy said.

Mrs Hope took Harold out very gently. He stayed rolled up tightly.

"That shows he's better, doesn't it?" Mandy said. "He didn't roll up when we first found him, because he was too weak."

Mrs Hope gently placed Harold on the scales. "He's certainly better now," she said, checking the reading. "A whopping 678 grammes. I'd say he's as fit as a fiddle!"

"Then we *can* take him to Gran and Grandad's?" Mandy felt really excited.

Mrs Hope laughed. "You'd better borrow a

pet carrier. There's one over there."

Mandy put some bedding into the cardboard carrier, then Mrs Hope put Harold inside. Mandy carried him into the kitchen, her face covered in smiles.

"Oh, excellent," James said. "Harold's going home!"

Grandad chuckled. "Any final tips about hedgehog care, Emily?"

Mrs Hope smiled. "You seem to be doing fine by yourself. I take it you found our hedgehog leaflet useful! I hope Harold likes his hedgehog home. Next time I come for a visit, I'll pop in and have a look at it."

"Hedgehog Home! That's a brilliant name for it, Mum!" Mandy said.

Gran was waiting at Lilac Cottage. As soon as Grandad stopped the car she came outside.

"Bring Harold straight through," Gran urged, holding the gate open. She followed Grandad, James and Mandy up the garden.

"Where's Blackie, Mrs Hope?" James asked.

"In the kitchen," Gran answered. "Playing with a dog chew. I only just managed to rescue one of my wooden spoons from him!"

Mandy and James laughed. Even *Gran* couldn't control Blackie all the time!

"Right." Grandad stood by the compost heap. "Have we thought of everything? Let's check."

Mandy looked at the fence-like enclosure around Grandad's compost heap. It had been like a big crate, with three sides. Now that Grandad had put planks of wood across the open end, it was transformed into a safe pen. Harold had lots of space for poking about in front of the compost heap. And there was the end of the drainpipe, sticking out of the heap itself.

"I think it will do very nicely," Gran said.

"Thank you, Dorothy," Grandad said, looking pleased.

"We've put down some peanuts," Mandy said. "Unroasted ones. The leaflet says the other sort are bad for hedgehogs."

"And some sultanas," James added. "And a bowl of water."

"Oh, look," Mandy said. "Where did that pile of straw come from?"

"I put it there," Gran admitted. She looked a bit embarrassed. "I found an old bag of it in the shed. I thought Harold could use it for his nest."

"What a good idea!" Mandy said. It looked like Gran had been reading the Animal Ark leaflet, too!

"Well, here goes." Grandad carefully opened the lid of the pet carrier. He reached inside and picked Harold up. "Gently does it. I'll tuck him under the straw: he'll feel safe there."

Mandy looked down at Harold. "He's curled into a tight ball," she remarked.

"I expect he needs to get used to things," Gran said. "Let's leave him alone for a little while."

Mandy was dying to stay and wait for Harold to uncurl. But she knew Gran was right.

"We can creep back later," James said. "Maybe he'll be exploring by then."

Mandy nodded. Then she followed everyone into the cottage. Now that there was time to relax, she remembered the emergency up at Syke Farm. She hoped the lamb would survive.

A drink of milk and huge slice of ginger cake later, Mandy pushed her chair back. "Thanks, Gran. That was lovely," she said.

"Yes, it certainly was," James said, licking crumbs from his lips.

Mandy glanced up at the kitchen clock. Half an hour had passed. She looked at James.

Grandad chuckled. "Come on, you two. Let's go outside and check on Harold now. I wouldn't like either of you to burst with impatience!"

They walked down the garden path in single file. Mandy first, then James, followed by Gran and Grandad. As they drew near the compost heap they heard noises.

"Oh." Mandy recognised the sound. "It's Harold eating!"

And sure enough, as they got nearer, they could see him snuffling back and forth. He nosed the food. He pawed at it. Then he began chomping the peanuts.

Grandad laughed softly. "He doesn't mind being watched at all."

When the food was all gone, Harold ran towards the compost heap and began scrabbling around at the base of it.

"Heavens!" Gran whispered. "I didn't realise hedgehogs had such long legs!"

"Oh yes," Mandy explained. "They can run

quite fast when they want to."

"When there's food about, you mean," James added.

Harold snitted the end of the drainpipe, then stuck his head inside it. Mandy held her breath. Would he go right inside? Slowly Harold moved forward; just his back legs were sticking out. Then he disappeared completely.

Grandad beamed with pleasure. "I think Harold likes his new home."

"He loves it!" Mandy said. "You are clever, Grandad. This house was all your idea."

Grandad gave her a cuddle. "You and James helped as well. And so did Gran. I'd say it was a joint effort!"

Late in the afternoon, Mandy, James and Grandad went back out into the garden for a final "spot of Harold-watching" as Gran called it, before they went home.

It was getting dark and the stars were out. The snow gave a ghostly light to the garden.

They were careful to make no sudden movements. At first there was no sign of Harold. Then, as they watched, a pointed nose poked out of the drainpipe. Little by little Harold emerged, his spines laid flat against his body.

"Oh." Mandy was delighted. "Isn't he clever? He's been exploring the inside of your buried crate again!"

"Yes," Grandad whispered. "He's been in and out of it all afternoon."

"He must be having a jolly good look around," James said.

Grandad grinned. "I expect hedgehogs are pretty choosy about where they build their nests."

"What's he doing now?" Mandy watched

Harold amble across to the pile of straw.

Harold picked up a mouthful of straw. He snuffled about, pawing at the edges of the compost heap. Now and then he stuck his head into the old drainpipe, but he didn't go back inside the crate.

"I don't think he's made his mind up yet!" Mandy said, as Harold dropped the straw. Then he trundled back to the pile of nesting material and began investigating it again.

Grandad took off his cap and scratched his head. "I've a feeling this could take a long time!"

8

A busy time

It was dark when Grandad dropped Mandy back at Animal Ark.

Mr and Mrs Hope were watching TV in the cosy sitting-room. Mandy threw herself into a chair. "Hi Mum, Dad! Guess what?"

Mr Hope gave her a tired smile. "I've no energy left for guessing, love. Why don't you just tell me?"

"OK." Mandy's head was full of fascinating

hedgehog details. She rushed on, telling her mum and dad all about Harold and how he adored his new home. And how he was building a new nest inside the crate buried in Grandad's compost heap.

"Slow down a bit, Mandy," Mrs Hope said. "Your dad's had a tiring day."

"Oh." Mandy bit her lip. "Sorry, Dad."

"It's all right, Mandy." Her dad reached over and patted her hand. "I've only just got back from Syke Farm. It was a difficult delivery — touch and go for a while, in fact."

"The lamb," Mandy gasped. "Is it . . . ?"

"Alive?" Mr Hope smiled and nodded. "But Snowflake's very small and weak, so Dora's taken her into the house to hand-rear her."

Mandy's eyes filled with tears. "Snowflake? What a lovely name." She had a sudden thought. "Dad! Snowflake's the first lamb of the year!"

"Breakfast!" Mrs Hope called.

Mandy hurried downstairs. She had barely slept a wink for worrying about Snowflake.

As she came into the kitchen Mr Hope was

finishing his toast. "I'll just go and give Syke Farm a quick phone call," he said.

Mandy was about to jump up and go after him, but Mrs Hope put a bowl of hot porridge on the table.

"Eat up, Mandy," she said. "Your dad will be back in two minutes. You can ask him about Snowflake then."

"OK, Mum." Mandy sighed. All she could think about was the tiny lamb.

"Mary comes home today, doesn't she?" Mrs Hope said. "Are you and James going over to Lilac Cottage to welcome her?"

Mandy nodded. "I'm meeting him and Blackie there."

Just then, her dad came back into the kitchen. Mandy looked up. She held her breath.

Mr Hope smiled. "Dora says Snowflake's drunk a little milk. And her mother's doing fine."

"Oh, good." Mandy let out a sigh of relief.

"Snowflake isn't out of danger yet," Mr Hope explained. "Don't get your hopes up, Mandy."

Mandy smiled. "I'll try not to," she said. But she still felt encouraged. Snowflake *had* made it through her first night.

"Almost time for surgery to start." Mr Hope slipped on his white coat. "See you later." He bent down to kiss Mandy on her cheek.

"Bye, Dad," Mandy said.

She finished her breakfast and put her dish in the sink. She was dying to tell James that the ewe had given birth safely. He had been worried about the lamb as well.

Mrs Hope came into the kitchen. She was carrying her vet's bag. "I'll drop you at Lilac Cottage if you're ready. My first call's out that way."

"OK, thanks, Mum." Mandy pulled on her boots, coat and scarf. She followed her mum outside and climbed into the Land Rover.

James was already at Lilac Cottage. He came to the front door, Blackie at his heels. They stood and waved to Mrs Hope as she drove away.

"What happened to Dora Janeki's injured ewe?" James asked worriedly.

"She had a little lamb!" Mandy said excitedly. "Isn't it great?" She told him all about Snowflake.

"Wow! Just think: the first lamb this year!"

James said, when Mandy had finished. "Will she be all right?"

"Dad says it's still touch and go," Mandy said. "But I just *know* she'll be fine. Let's go inside and tell Gran and Grandad about Snowflake!"

They found Grandad sorting out glass jars and paper for recycling. The whole cottage smelled wonderful: Gran had obviously been up baking since the crack of dawn.

"Hi, Grandad," Mandy said. "Where's Gran?"

"She's upstairs, getting the spare bedroom ready for Mary," Grandad replied.

"But I thought it *was* ready," Mandy said.

"Not according to your Gran!" Grandad smiled.

Mandy had just finished telling him about Snowflake when Gran came into the kitchen. "There's a taxi outside!" she called. "It must be Mary!"

"We'd best go and welcome her, then," Grandad said.

They all went outside. Just climbing out of the taxi was a lady with grey hair. Gran gave her a hug. "Welcome to your temporary home!"

Mary was a small woman with bright-blue

eyes. She smiled warmly at Mandy and James. "Dorothy tells me you've been taking good care of Frisky."

"We've loved looking after him, haven't we, James?" Mandy said.

James nodded.

"Come on inside, Mary," Gran said, ushering her friend through the gate. "I'll put the kettle on."

Mandy and James helped Grandad take Mary's suitcases upstairs. They put them in the spare bedroom.

"Oh, look," Mandy said. "Frisky's awake!"

And he was. He was sitting up and looking out of the cage, and he didn't look the least bit sleepy.

"That's strange," James said. "He's hardly ever awake in the daytime."

"It's as if he knows Mary's back," Mandy said.

"Perhaps he does," came a voice from behind them. Mary stood in the doorway. She came straight up to the cage. "Hello, Frisky. Have you missed me?"

Frisky came right up to the bars. He stretched upwards, balancing on his back feet and showing his pale tummy. His little pink nose sniffed at the air.

"Well, well," Grandad said. "I've never seen him do *that* before."

"It means he wants to come out," Mary explained. She opened the cage door and put her hand inside.

Frisky hopped straight on to her palm. Mary took him out of the cage and stroked him very gently. "Hello, Frisky," she said softly. "My, my – you do look well."

Frisky twitched his whiskers. Then he cocked his head to one side, as if he really was listening to Mary.

Grandad chuckled. "Just look at that!"

Mandy and James laughed, too. But underneath, Mandy couldn't help feeling just a bit sad: she would really miss looking after Frisky.

"Frisky hopped straight on to Mandy's hand once," James said.

"Did he?" Mary asked, looking surprised. She smiled at Mandy. "He usually only does that for me. He must really have enjoyed his holiday here."

Mandy brightened. "Can we still come and visit him?" she asked.

"Of course you can," Mary said. "Every day if you want to. I'm going to be sharing this bedroom with Frisky for some time!"

They all laughed.

Mary held out her cupped hands. Frisky looked up at Mandy, his jet-black eyes blinking.

"Would you like to hold him?" Mary said.

Mandy's face broke into a grin. "Oh, yes, please!"

"So, then Mandy saw the tracks in the

snow . . ." Grandad was saying to Mary later that morning. "And that's how we found Harold."

They all sat around the table enjoying the special "welcome home" treats. There was strawberry jam and cream to go with Gran's scones. And a fluffy sponge cake with coffee icing.

"Well!" Mary said. "This is a *very* special tea break. Aren't I lucky? And Frisky and Harold are safe and sound. All I have to worry about now is a silly old damp cottage!"

Mandy chuckled. She was liking Mary more and more. "Can we show Mary Harold's new home now, please?"

Grandad finished drinking his tea. He stood up. "Why not? I'll come outside with you and James. I need to pop into my greenhouse anyway."

Gran smiled at Mary. "I don't know who's more interested in Harold – Mandy and James, or Tom!"

"Well, hedgehogs *are* fascinating, Gran!" Mandy said. "Aren't they, James?"

James nodded.

"Quite right." Mary reached for her coat. "I

can't wait to see this Hedgehog Home. I've
heard so much about it."

9

Harold-watching

Over the next couple of days, Mandy and James were busy. They took Blackie for walks. They met up with Gary Roberts and Pam Stanton and went tobogganing. And they went to visit Frisky. They had been checking up on Harold too, but all was quiet around Hedgehog Home.

"Frisky really loves his exercise wheel, doesn't he?" Mandy said. "Gran says she can hear it squeaking away half the night!"

She was sitting on the chair in Lilac Cottage's spare bedroom. James was perched on the end of the bed. They were chatting to Mary while she cleaned out Frisky's cage.

Mary nodded. "I missed hearing that sound while I was staying with my sister," she said with a smile.

"And he loves chewing on his piece of apple wood," James added.

"That's right. It wears down his teeth." Mary began spreading clean shavings on the bottom of Frisky's cage. "There's never a dull moment when you have a pet to look after!"

"No," James agreed. "Benji and Blackie keep me busy!"

Mandy smiled. Even though she didn't have a pet of her own, there was always something going on at Animal Ark.

"Almost finished," Mary said. "I'm just going to put a dab of cooking oil on that squeaky wheel. Would you like to see to Frisky's food and water?"

"Yes, please!" Mandy and James chorused. They hurried off to wash the little china bowl and water bottle and find the bag of hamster mix.

"There," Mary said closing the cage door a few minutes later. "The hamster's house has had a wash-and-brush-up! And once he wakes up it'll be 'Frisky has a field day'!"

Mandy and James laughed. They liked Mary's habit of playing with words.

"Hello." Mary glanced out of the bedroom window. "Your grandad's Harold-watching again."

Mandy and James went over to the window. Grandad looked up and saw them. He began waving his arms about.

"I think he wants us to go outside," James said.

"I bet Harold's finished building his nest!" Mandy said excitedly.

"Let's go and have a look," James said.

When Mandy, James and Mary got to the pen, Gran was already there with Grandad. "What's all this fuss about, Tom?" she was asking. "There's nothing to see."

"Aha," Grandad said. "Not now, there's not. That's because Harold's asleep in his cosy new nest. Do you want to have a look at it?"

"But – how can we?" Mandy asked.

"I thought the only way into the crate was

through that drainpipe," James said.

"Uh-huh," Grandad said. He winked at James. Removing a couple of planks of wood, he climbed carefully into Harold's pen.

Mandy frowned. Grandad had a mysterious look on his face. What was he up to? She watched as he bent down and began carefully to scoop away the compost.

Very gently, he dug out a small hollow. Then he stopped and straightened up. Mandy's eyes widened. There was something there. It was a tight ball of hay and torn-up newspaper.

"Oh," she gasped. "It's Harold's new nest!"

"Yes," James said. "But just look where it is!"

"It's right *next* to Grandad's old crate," Mandy said.

She was dying to laugh, but she managed not to. Grandad must have been really disappointed. He had taken so much trouble with burying the crate and fixing on the drainpipe.

"How did you know where the nest was, Grandad?" she asked.

"I did a bit of detective work," Grandad said. "Before I went to bed last night I popped outside, just to see how Harold was getting on. I shone my torch and saw him – digging away like mad into the side of my compost heap!" He gave a sniff. "Don't know what he's got against my special, deluxe Hedgehog Home. Cheeky little beggar!"

Gran began to chuckle. "Dear me! The look on your face, Tom!"

James and Mary joined in with the laughter. Even though Mandy tried really hard not to laugh, she couldn't help it.

Suddenly Grandad's face split in a huge grin. "I suppose the little chap's got a right to choose his own home!" he said, wiping his eyes. "That's one determined little hedgehog! I'm going to miss having him around."

Mandy and James helped Grandad to cover Harold's nest back up.

"Brrr," Gran said. "I can smell snow in the air. Let's all go into the house. Mandy, James, are you ready for some hot chocolate?"

"Ooh, yes please," they said at once.

"I think you're right about that snow." Grandad rubbed his hands together. "I'll just nip into the greenhouse, then I'll be in to join you."

The kitchen was warm and cosy after the garden. Mandy and James sat at the table. Gran poured milk into a saucepan and Mary set out the cups. Suddenly, the back door opened and Grandad rushed inside.

"The heater's packed up!" he cried. "What am I going to do? I could lose all my fuchsias."

"Oh, no," Gran said. "I was afraid of this."

Grandad scratched his head. "You were right all along, Dorothy. I should have listened to you."

"Never mind that now," Gran said. "We'd better think of something — and quick!"

"I've no idea where you'd buy a greenhouse heater in Welford village," Mary said.

Mandy wished she could help. Suddenly she remembered something. "Isn't there a new garden shop in Walton?"

"Yes," James said. "It opened last week. Mum and Dad have been. They said it's huge!"

Grandad's face lit up. "Gosh, I'd forgotten about that place! Well done, you two!" He dashed off to find the phone book.

A few moments later, they heard Grandad on the phone. "I see," he was saying. "Yes, I'll do that. Thanks. Goodbye."

"Well?" Gran asked, as he came back into the room.

"No luck, I'm afraid," Grandad said. "The shop's had trouble with deliveries in the bad weather. I've had to order a heater; it won't arrive for a day or two."

"Hmm," Mary said thoughtfully. "You don't need a lot of heat to keep the frost out of a greenhouse,"

"That's true," Gran said. "I've just had an idea!"

She hurried across the kitchen. Opening a cupboard, she began fishing about at the back. A moment later, she passed Mandy a plastic bag. "Hold on to these for me, love."

In the bag were loads of small white candles. Each one sat inside its own small metal cup. "What are these, Gran?" Mandy asked.

"They're night-lights," Gran explained. "They burn for a long time." She ducked back into the cupboard and dragged out a dusty box full of empty tins. "And if we put some in these tins, *they*'ll give out a bit of heat, as well."

"Heat?" Grandad jumped up. "Dorothy, I reckon that might just work, you know."

"Of course it will." Gran smiled. "I wasn't

in the Girl Guides for nothing!" She gave him one of her looks. "It's a good thing you insisted on keeping this box full of old tin cans!"

Grandad gave her a kiss on the cheek. "You see! It's best not to throw anything away – you never know when it might be useful!"

Mandy and James grinned. Even Gran couldn't argue with that!

Outside in the greenhouse, everyone helped set out the tin cans. Grandad had used bent wire to make hangers for some of them, and Mandy hung these up around the greenhouse.

"Lighting-up time!" Grandad said.

"Ooh," Mandy said, a few minutes later, looking at the tiny lights glimmering inside their shiny silver tins. "They look so pretty."

"Just like Christmas lanterns!" James said.

"They're the best lanterns ever." Grandad smiled. He was back to his old cheerful self. "And they'll do the job very nicely – until my new heater arrives."

10

A family move

Mandy ticked another day off on her wildlife calendar. It hung on her bedroom wall, next to an animal poster.

It was Friday – almost the end of the holiday. But Mandy had more on her mind than school on Monday.

"Six days old!" she sang to herself as she brushed her hair. The lamb was still on her mind as she went into Animal Ark reception. "Snowflake's six days old!" she said to Jean Knox.

The receptionist was checking the appointment book. Surgery was starting in ten minutes. She looked up and smiled. "Snowflake? That's the premature lamb up at Syke Farm, isn't it?"

"Yep!" Mandy said. "Dad's been keeping an eye on her."

Just then Mrs Hope came out of the unit. She was holding a grey cat.

"Your dad's going to see Snowflake tomorrow," Mrs Hope said. "If you ask him nicely, he might let you and James tag along."

"Oh," Mandy said. "That would be brilliant!" She looked at the little grey cat. "Aren't you lovely," she said, stroking the cat's head very gently. "What's its name, Mum?"

"Her name's Dusty," Mrs Hope said, with a smile.

"What's wrong with her?" Mandy asked. She felt a bit sad, just like she always did when animals were sick.

"Oh, she's not sick," Mrs Hope replied. "Dusty's having an operation today to stop her having kittens."

Mandy stroked the cat's soft fur. She knew that animals recovered quickly from these

operations. "I only came in to say goodbye," she said to her mum. "Gran's picking James up, then calling for me. She'll be here in a minute."

"Oh, yes. You're all going to Cowslip Cottage, aren't you?" Mrs Hope said.

Mandy nodded. "The machine from Mars has dried everything out," she joked. "Some workmen have been and put heating in now, too. Mary wants to move back in tomorrow."

"The *what* machine?" Jean said, raising her eyebrows.

Mrs Hope chuckled. "I'll tell you later. Make

sure you wear your wellies, Mandy. Now the snow is beginning to melt, everything's wet underfoot."

Mandy nodded. It was definitely warmer outside. There was only a skin of ice on the puddles in the lane now. Fat drops of water were sliding off the trees and you could see bits of grass poking through the snow.

Mandy dashed off to find her wellies. Then she poked her head round the door into reception. "Gran's here. Got to go. Bye Mum, bye Jean! See you later!"

As she shot out of the surgery, she heard Jean Knox's laugh. "Goodness! Was that Mandy, or was it a comet?"

Gran and Mary were inside Cowslip Cottage. They were hanging curtains. Mandy and James had been trying to help, but Blackie kept getting under everyone's feet.

"That pup's got too much energy!" Gran said. "Has he had a walk today?"

James shook his head. "Only a little one. I was going to take him out a bit later."

"How about . . . now?" Gran suggested with a grin.

"OK," James said, going a bit red.

"Come on, James," Mandy said. "We can take him into the garden."

"Good idea," Gran said behind them. "Let him wear himself out."

First Blackie scampered around on the lawn. Then he attacked an empty plastic flowerpot. Finally he poked his nose under the roots of the old apple-tree.

"It's a good thing the flood water's drained away," Mandy said, laughing at the puppy's antics.

"He'll get his head stuck in a minute!" James knelt down and pulled Blackie away. "Come out, Blackie! Oh, look. It's all dry inside here now that the snow's thawed out."

Mandy nodded. "Grandad said that's because the apple-tree's growing on the side of a slight slope."

"So Harold was pretty clever, wasn't he?" James said. "He picked a really good place to build his nest."

"Yes," Mandy agreed. "But he didn't expect the pipe to burst!"

They both chuckled.

"Grandad's bringing Harold back

tomorrow," Mandy said, when they'd stopped laughing. "He said Mary's family could all move back here together."

"Mary's family?" James said.

"Yes," Mandy said. "Mary, Frisky . . . and Harold!"

"Fancy old Harold building his nest *outside* your grandad's buried crate!" James said. "I bet any other hedgehog would have loved Hedgehog Home."

Mandy nodded. "But Harold isn't just any old hedgehog!"

"No," James said, with a grin.

They watched Blackie as he finished sniffing under the bushes. Suddenly he raced back to the lawn and began tearing around the apple-tree. His ears were laid back against his head as he ran in circles.

Mandy giggled. "I think we can go back inside soon. Blackie seems to be doing a good job of wearing himself out!"

Mandy and James looked out of the windows as the Land Rover climbed the winding roads. It was early the following morning. Snow still lay thick up on the high moors.

"All right, you two?" her dad asked.

Mandy and James nodded. Mandy felt excited as the Land Rover drew to a halt in front of the farmhouse. A thin woman came out to meet them.

"Good morning, Dora," Mr Hope said. "How's Snowflake?"

"Morning, vet." Dora Janeki looked at Mandy and James. "Why don't you come inside and see for yourselves?"

"She's not very friendly, is she?" James whispered.

"Not to people," Mandy said. "But she really loves her sheep."

Mandy and James followed Mr Hope into the farmhouse's warm back kitchen. A wooden box was placed near to the old-fashioned range. There was a blanket inside.

"Here she is," Dora said.

Mandy and James looked where she was pointing. At first the box seemed empty. Then the blanket moved and a head appeared.

"Oh." Mandy got her first glimpse of the tiny lamb. "Isn't she beautiful?"

"Yes, she is," James agreed.

Dora Janeki looked pleased. "You can watch

me give her a bottle if you like."

"Yes, please!" Mandy and James said together.

Dora bent down and picked up the wrapped bundle. "Would you like to hold her while I warm the milk?"

Mandy nodded. She was enchanted by the tiny lamb. Snowflake had a black nose and soft brown eyes. "She's the sweetest thing I've ever seen," she said, cuddling her.

Suddenly Snowflake opened her mouth. "Baa–aa. Baa–aa," she cried.

"Crikey!" James said. "That's loud for such a tiny lamb."

"Yes." Mr Hope chuckled. "That's a healthy, hungry cry!"

Mandy brushed her cheek against Snowflake's woolly head. It felt so soft and warm. "Oh, Dad." Her eyes were shining. "Snowflake's all right now, isn't she?"

Mr Hope nodded. "A healthy little girl. The first lamb of the year!"

Mandy was walking on air. She had told everyone about Snowflake – her mum, her grandparents, Mary.

"There's only Frisky left to tell," Grandad said. "And I don't think *he* could care less!"

They were all in Cowslip Cottage's garden. It was time for Harold to move back to his old nest site.

Grandad carefully opened the pet carrier. It was filled with crumbly dark compost. Buried inside it was Harold's nest.

Grandad lifted out the ball of straw and newspaper and put it gently under the apple-tree's roots. Then he packed a thick layer of compost all around it.

"We don't want to wake Harold up just yet," he said. "Although I expect he'll be out and about in a day or so."

"I'm sure he will," Mary said. "This warmer weather will bring him out."

"Well, there we are," Grandad said. "Harold's safe and sound."

"Just like Mary and Frisky!" Mandy said.

Mary gave her a hug. "It's lovely to be back in my *dry* cottage. And Harold's back in his own dry home."

Everyone laughed. Mandy looked at James. "Back in his *proper* Hedgehog Home!" they said together.